Lesbian Humor Is Not an Oxymoron

Light Verse

By

Sandra de Helen

A Launch Point Press Trade Paperback Original

ISBN 978-1-63304-2162
eBook ISBN 978-1-63304-2186

FIRST EDITION: First Printing, 2019

Formatting: Patty Schramm
Cover Design: Lorelei

Portland, Oregon
www.LaunchPointPress.com

Praise for Sandra de Helen's
Desire Returns for a Visit

"These are fresh poems in every sense of the word. Flirty, audacious, original. A fresh take on Dickinson's love of women and words. A brazen exploration of the life cycle of love affairs. This book is an open-mouthed kiss to the reader. It will leave you breathless."
~G.L. Morrison, poet, lover of words, and writer of short fiction

"[Sandra de Helen's] book of poems is a great way to read a truthful, witty, poignant memoir of lesbian love."
~Judy Grahn, poet, author, professor, and grande dame of lesbian poetry and nonfiction

"I didn't need to read beyond the first line of the first poem to know I'd be loving this book."
~Lee Lynch, novelist, essayist, short story writer, trailblazer, and both the inspiration and first winner of the annual Lee Lynch Classic Award given by the Golden Crown Literary Society

To Kate Kasten who inspired me
(no, commanded me)
to write funny.

Author's Foreword

If we can't laugh at ourselves, who can we laugh at? No one, because that's not politically correct.

Sandra de Helen
December 2019

Contents

ON A PERSONAL NOTE

ANIMALS

Because Goats

Capricorn, born on the cusp of
Aquarius. That's me.

Mom had a pet goat when they
were both kids. Mom would get on

her tricycle and ride round and
round the outside of her grandmother's

house, the goat wearing a cow bell
running alongside her.

When she grew up, she had me,
a kid who only thought she was

a goat. When put down for a nap, I
climbed the dresser reaching for my doll

Susie. The drawer knob came off, the
screw made a hole in my knee.

Mom came to my rescue. Poor little kid.
I still have the scar.

When I reached puberty, I discovered
my goat nature included more than

scaling cliffs and eating peanut shells.
Boys, girls, the bed post—I climbed them all.

I still have the scars.

Snakes are the Devil, am I right?

How do you suppose the snake got such a
bad reputation? Other than the bible, I
mean. It must have already been, like

wicked bad, for the guy who wrote
Genesis to make the snake the devil.
I mean, snakes are kind of slithery and

all that, but they aren't slimy. They don't
carry rabies. They don't even growl.
So who did they piss off to become

the scum of the universe? And what
could they possibly have done? It's
like nobody would've been forever scared

out of their pants if all a snake did was
offer Eve a bite of an apple. An apple
she already wanted, you know? I'm

thinking maybe the deal was that snakes
reminded guys of their willies, except
grown up snakes were fatter and longer

than any guy's Johnson. So there was
that envy thing. Plus some snakes are
poisonous, so that's like powerful, you

know what I mean? The worst a guy
could do with his pecker is spread
disease and they didn't even know that

back in the olden days. 'Cause, let's face
it, there was like nothing but wildlife
back in the day. And some of it was

super scary. Wolverines? I mean, come
on. They'd make a great Satan. And
what if the whole story was Eve and

Adam from the get go. And women
were super self-conscious about their
vaginas? Would the tempter have been

a clam? Would clams then have had bad
reputations? I'm just saying.

Salmonella

Shelley Bell got salmonella
not from eggs, like you might think

but from her strange bedfellow
she plucked from the drink

twenty years ago and
made her bee eff eff.

i know! right?
and every night

they sleep together
side by side

leg by leg by leg
leg leg—leg.

Her "friend"
is a turtle this big!

I mean it's huge!
I think she kissed it.

Shelley Bell got salmonella.
What do you think?

Good Intentions

I wanted to rescue those kittens,
provide a good home, but I was
short-sighted. Couldn't afford the
vet bills.

I swore I'd be a better mother than
my own. But I set the bar too low.

My life is filled with stories of
my good intentions. I'm headed
straight for hell.

Seven Cats

Seven cats makes a girl happy.
Six can make a person seem obsessive

if you aren't careful with selection. It's important
to have at least one Maine Coon, two calico cats,

one kitten, and two tabbies if you can only have six.
Otherwise you might lose your credibility. For instance

six Siamese would cause your neighbors to call 911
every time one of them goes into heat. The cats, not

the neighbors. You got that, right? Manx wouldn't do,
not six Manx. Not six of anything, even Maine Coon.

Too much cat hair for one thing, you wouldn't have time
to do anything but brush your cats. So, two Maine Coons,

two tabbies, one kitten of any kind really, and two
calico cats is a combo to make any girl happy.

In the Mood for Wooly

The bunnies are soft, and they have
pretty eyes, but may I see something
that walks? I don't think I'm in the
market for a hopping animal. Ooh,

this little fainting goat is really cute,
wait, why is it lying down? I can't
be having a pet that faints. Too bad,

though. Oh well, what else do you
have back there? I'm in the mood for
wooly, I think. Nothing that sheds.

I love big eyes, long eyelashes, and
long legs too. Sheep are just not
my thing. Cats are fine as far as

being self-reliant and furry. But
can you ride one? No. That reminds
me, I want one I can ride if I feel

like it. No thanks on the camel. It's
too big. I want to be able to take it
out on my balcony to show it off.

Llamas? You mean Buddhist
priests? Heavens, no. Oh, I see.
Well then, certainly. Send them in.

WORDS AND MEANINGS

We Are Not Girls

A butch, a trans woman, and a femme walk into
a bar. Gay bartender says, What'll it be, girls?

They all draw back, draw in breath to protest,
as he points behind him to the large sparkly

pink sign: Ladies' Night, Margaritas 2 for 1.
Then in unison, they speak: Margarita, please.

OMG So Cute LOL

May I make a suggestion? It may seem
peculiar, but if you'll stay with me, I
think you might like it.

Don't think I'm pushy. If you don't
take my advice, I won't have hurt
feelings, I promise.

Remember, free advice is worth what
you pay for it. It's like when they tell
you not to throw the baby out with
the bath water.

Has anyone ever done that? I rest my
case. So, here's what I'm thinking. You
are participating in a steeple chase on
Saturday, right?

Your horse would look adorable in a
poodle costume. I saw one on Facebook
and immediately thought of you.

The True Meaning of Xyst

A garden walk, planted with trees, or
a covered portico, a promenade. I
think not. This is a word created

for the express purpose of using it in
Scrabble when you're in a tight spot.
No space for exigencies, or Excalibur,

no room for xylophone (as if!) or
other impressive words. This is
for when the only vowel you have

is Y, there is room for only four
letters, and of course, let's throw in
an X. The S means you can add

on the word as a possessive to your
jealous opponent's ZEBRA.
Xyst is worth more than points.

Logomachy, or a dispute over words

Who has words over words? More people
than you might imagine. Better to stick to
Words With Friends, may the best friend

win. In this game, you can guess at words.
If you're right, the word is posted, points
are awarded, and you move on. If you're

wrong, WWF tells you your word is
unacceptable. Are you seriously going
to argue with an electronic game?

Alec Baldwin got into trouble because of
Words With Friends. He wouldn't shut off
his phone in first class on the airplane,

because he was trying to come up with the
right word for his game. Instead he came
up with some choice words for the flight
attendant.

He landed in hot water.

It is Always Now

It is always now, and yet it is never now
because according to scientists and neurologists,

now is not even possible. Now is already gone,
tomorrow comes and goes, yesterday is always a memory

but memories are never real, so all we have is now, which
    is never here,
so what do we have at all?

All we have is our perception of now so we had better
    learn to grasp it as
best we can, and that is all we have. Perception is all we
    can change.
And change is all we can count on.

A Letter

"Going to him! Happy letter! Tell him—
. . . Until to-morrow,—happy letter!
Gesture, coquette, and shake your head!"
~Emily Dickinson

Blue balloons encapsulate my missives of twenty words or
    less.
I could write more but most recipients wouldn't read past
    five

I withhold adjectives, use emojis to express my deepest
    feelings—
hearts, smiling faces, purple cats, alien heads—I don't
    know what

I'm saying, but you respond with five mice and a cloud, so
    I think
we're communicating. Once in my lifetime I wrote to
    family, friends,

even pen pals. I wrote to editors, I wrote formal
    complaints—I received letters
in response almost daily. I sent Valentine cards to
    everyone I loved in any way.

I had scrapbooks filled with Christmas cards received
    from those
I had sent handmade, handwritten cards—I wrote
    postcards

as if they were short stories and hoped my friends would
save them for the day
my autograph became valuable. Letters died out before I
    did. Email came along,

dragging all of us into the new millennium—editors had
    to decide whether to capitalize
the first letter of the new word email, or whether to add an
    a hyphen while the rest of us

struggled with basic etiquette—how many colleagues did
    you insult your first year
with email? One of my co-workers was fired when he sent
    a birth announcement

to All—and crashed the company computer because the
    system wasn't prepared
for enthusiasm. Now we message, tweet, or leave
    voicemail—even

the telephone is being left behind. With the rise of smart
    watches, soon one letter
may be all we need.

Part Time Witch

It's seasonal, this carousing. Only when
the leaves turn, the wind kicks up,

the neighbors decorate for Halloween.
Only then do I begin to conjure. Rocking,

shocking, I call up the spirits. Together
we dance in the moonlight, join our

voices in howling, dragging the iron
cauldron to the clearing, where we

bob for apples until
the sun comes up.

CHICKENS

Damn Chicken

It's you and that damn chicken again.
What is it with you and that hen?

I could see her attraction for you if she
implanted on you or whatever the cuss you call it,

but why are you so hung up on her? Is it
because she lays eggs and you don't anymore?

Or is it just because she cackles and you can't?
Is it because she's a dominecker and you're a brunette?

Well, then, what? Just tell me because I am never going to
     stop
asking what is it with you and that damn chicken?

Chickens

It has yet to occur to the chickens that they can't
talk. They bring up the sun every day of the
world. They lay eggs that bring happiness to the

household, and sometimes new baby chickens to
the farm. They create manure, which enriches
gardens. Their feathers make great dusters, and

doesn't everything good taste like chicken? Not
that they are martyrs, no. They are realists. And if they
could talk, they would speak about all they do, all they feel,

all they think. The roosters would crow on
about politics, fueled as they are by their
testosterone. The hens would no doubt

create mommy vlogs, clucking about this and
that, including politics because mommies leave
out nothing. Spinster chicks would have their

own websites, putting up videos about matters
which ruffle their feathers, and leaving the
rest of us with egg on our faces.

World without Chickens, Amen

Glory be to the Mother Hen, and to
her daughter, Pullet, and to the
Holy Shit we're only pheasants.

As it was in the beginning, is now,
and ever shall be.

World without chickens. Amen.

Now, who wants to play
pheasant?

How a Lesbian is Like a Chicken

She clucks over her peeps, scratches in
the dirt for a tidbit, gets her feathers
ruffled when the cock crows.

She also has eggs, and may lay one
if the mood
suits her.

A lesbian/chicken will flock with her
hens, cackling, pecking, sharing the
food with her sisters and other chicks.

Feminists don't like the word chicks
for women. Not all feminists
are lesbians, as once thought. Of course, not

all lesbians are feminists either.
Lesbians, like chickens,
nest. Feathering

their homes with tomes on how to be
in the world. With a giggle
and a gaggle,

they live with one eye looking out for a
good place to light after a short flight, and
wee hens to call their friends.

HOW TO DO STUFF

How to Photograph the Moon

Early in the day, check the calendar. Make sure
it isn't the new moon. Then check the weather.

If the sky is overcast, don't waste your time.
In the afternoon, take a nap, so you'll be

rested and ready for a good long moon
party. When you wake up, have an energy bar,

maybe some caffeine, and
start laying out everything you'll need:

camera, lenses, memory disks, and be
sure your battery is charged. Polish

your lenses. Before twilight, bathe
yourself in warm rainwater, including

your hair. Shampoo with moonflower
extract, and rinse with dew gathered

at dawn. Dress yourself in clothing of
midnight blue, layers and layers if the

weather demands it, otherwise as few
as possible. Tiptoe up to the top of the

highest hill, and snap every few
minutes until the moon
bids you go home.

Lesbian Humor is Not an Oxymoron

How to Laugh:
Snicker.
Chuckle.
Guffaw.
Wheeze with a smile on your face.
Throw your head back and let her rip.

Why to Laugh:
Studies show laughter might
lengthen your life,
protect your heart,
fill you with endorphins,
and will definitely
relax your whole body.
Life can be brutal,
we may as well laugh.

Where to Laugh:
Wherever there is humor
or surprise.
In a theater, especially at live performances.
In the car.
In bed. Cats can be funny.
Dogs too.
Even your life partner can be funny.
You might even amuse yourself.

When to Laugh:
When someone says something that catches you by
    surprise.
When a baby smiles.
When your lover farts.
When your dog farts.
When your cat farts.

When Not to Laugh:
When you've made someone cry.
At a funeral.
To be polite.
Alone in public, unless you're wearing earbuds.

How to Give Directions

Tilt way back in your chair on the porch
take a draw on your corncob pipe

scratch your chin or your head or
your leg through your overalls

and say Yep. Then smack your
lips and swallow a couple of

times and knit your brow and
gaze off into the distance and

say Where's that again, young
fella? Even if the fella is a gal

even if you are younger than he
or she or they. Milk it. They are lost.

They need you. If they get impatient,
speed up just a little, pull them back in.

Say that's easy, you're practically
there. Ask them if they want

a drink of water. Ask them to
sit on the porch a spell. Tell

them they got a right pretty
vehicle. Ask them if they've got

a map. If they do, spread it out
completely, and smooth

the wrinkles plumb out of it.
Look at it every which way.

Point out to them where
they are. See if you can find

where they are supposed to be.
Then finally, in a simple way,

tell them how to get there,
offer to write it down.

Ask if they want to make a
phone call. Stay for supper.

Stay overnight. Watch the
moon come up at least?

Wave goodbye as they drive away.
Fold up their map real careful-like

in case they come back.
Try to remember the last time

anyone came for a visit.
Or even for directions.

How Do You Cope?

You can't quite grasp how to place direct object pronouns
in a sentence of Italian once you start messing about with
    tenses
plurals and so on unless you're actually in a classroom

and everyone else started weeks ahead of you.
What were you thinking?

You join a theatre company without ever going to a
    meeting
of the principals and you sit in a chair typing pages and
    pages

of names you can barely see and you agree to do
    something
you don't quite remember how to do.

Meanwhile the sun is shining and what you want to do
is work in the garden after how many days of rain so far
    this year?

Your garden club is meeting when and you are supposed
    to what
and your friends are waiting for visits and calls and you
    feel left out

and you have forgotten how to deal. You don't drink
you don't smoke you've given up sugar and all other
    forms of fun.

What is your coping method again?

Something to Pluck

A pianoforte, an organ, mandolin, guitar or banjo
xylophone, lyre, an old autoharp.

Pluck your eyebrows, chin or nose hair
or your girlfriend's chin or nose hair.
Pluck ideas out of thin air,

But for Pete's sake — Have
something to pluck. It's
National Stop Smoking Day.

Comfortable?

You sleep in my bed, drop your socks on my floor,
drink from my mug, sit in my chair at the table.

Read the morning Times before I get up and leave it
    unfolded in
a heap beside my couch after you do half the crossword
    puzzle in ballpoint.

Wrong answer. All guests should be comfortable but you
    are not at home.
You are in my home welcomed as a favored friend.

I'd be more comfortable if you
acted like one.

How to Deal with Bad Neighbors

I don't know how to deal with bad neighbors
so I treat them the same as the good ones.

I knock on their doors and hand them a plate of
cheesecake. I offer treats for their horrible

barking dogs. When they are in the throes of
a loud argument, and I fear for one of their

lives, I pound on the door, and ask them for
a cup of sugar.

In the city, in an apartment, where the trains
blare long, loud honks twenty-five times

a day and fifteen times at night, where the
lights never go off, and the walls of the building

are as concrete and sad-colored as the walls
of a prison, neighbors can't help

but be bad sometimes. But, just as when
the earth quakes, or fire catches, or a tsunami

threatens, neighbors can transmogrify
into heroes.

Maybe the way to treat bad neighbors is to act as
if we know disaster is coming

and we might need them to rescue us.

How to Get Your Friends to Trust You

Listen with all your heart, look into the
eyes of your friend and see what secrets
lie there, but never ask and never tell.

Stand up for your buddy whether you
were at the scene or not. Believe in her.

When the coach says the team won't
play until the person who wrote

"I am Big Pussy, Eat Me" on the coach's
office blackboard confesses, be the

first to say: I am, coach. I am
Big Pussy. If the rest of the team

didn't see the movie Spartacus you
will sit the season out, but your
friends will trust you.

ENVIRONMENT

A Postcard to the Red Planet

Dear Stranger from Outer Space,
Greetings from one sentient being

to another. I wouldn't know you were
here if another of my kind hadn't

boiled you in order to see what
temperatures you could withstand.

I hope you are one who escaped the
torture. I hope you have come in peace

As a redhead myself, I'm not one who
believes red means warlike. Your

color is of no concern to me. Your
reason for visiting is. If you have

come here to study us, please know
that we do not withstand high or low

temperatures. Some of us indulge our
curiosity by writing.
All best, A Poet

Reduce, Reuse, Recycle

If you wear your paper plates as garments on a
regular basis, you are proving you're body positive.
You will also probably get more dates

than you might otherwise. Save the Earth while you're
at it. Around the house you can go without clothing
all together. Hang up your garments the minute

you come in the door, wear them again and again.
Shower in twos. Save water and keep your love
life alive. Brush your teeth while showering.

Buy classic clothes you can wear forever.
Then do so. Trade with your boyfriend for a fun
time and to add a bit of mystery to your lives. You

know he looks better in your pink cashmere scarf
than you do. But you rock those black tux pants
so it all works out.

Just remember to slip into a little something
before you answer the front door
when company comes.

She Wore Rubber Gloves

My righteous predecessor in this kitchen used to
formulate recipes using almost nothing but
pecans, chemical elements, and food items grown

onsite. She worked with vigor, producing
pies, candy, even a pecan brandy which would
push you to drink beyond your norm.

Eventually, she expired. The true cause of her
demise was never known, but it was postulated
she substituted her own oxygen in a recipe for

photosynthesis and created an
overabundance of CO_2.

RELATIONSHIPS
OF ALL SORTS

Marriage

One too many times, I tied the
knot. I regretted my commitment
the day I made it. Saw an attorney

three days later begging for an
annulment he said I couldn't get.
Later I filed for divorce and got it.

The decree came with an
incorrect name for the man I had
left. I asked my attorney, who did

I actually divorce? His answer:
anyone you please. To be safe,
I never married again.

Fair Weather Friends

My Texan friends arrived for a visit one
day in February. I was new to Oregon

myself, having arrived July 4th to a
dusting of ash, a cold house I'd rented

without seeing, and had soon learned where
the furnace was and how to ignite it. Seven

months later, I thought I knew how the
weather worked: it would stay the same

all day. The Texans wanted to see the Pacific
Ocean, of course. So off we went to the coast.

Day started out bright and sunny.
We arrived to showers and wind. Never mind,

we had rain gear. We all jumped out of
the van, trekked down the beach, and were

lost from each other, one by one. I found cover
under a cardboard box and watched the grasses

go flat from the force of the wind.
When the wind changed direction, I headed
for shelter in the Chevy.

No sign of any of my friends. After what seemed
like an hour, they pulled themselves inside the vehicle,

soaked and more than a bit aggravated that
I was so wrong about the forecast.

I should have seen which way the
wind was blowing:

they've never been back.

Rapture 2011

Dear Kate,

I've been so busy that I didn't realize the Rapture was coming in FOUR DAYS. Are you ready? I'm just overwhelmed! I have so many questions, and I don't know where to turn for answers. I've been tweeting and posting on my Facebook timeline, but so far no one has responded. I asked whether Harold Camping has an 800 number and whether he is the right person to ask, but again: no answers. It's like nobody really cares about non-believers. But we are the ones who are going to be left behind to deal with everything until the world ends in October.

I'm worried about whether I can garden or not. What will happen to the weather? Is it going to be the same, can I just go ahead and garden like last year and expect that my lettuce will rot in the ground from all the rain and then the tomatoes will overtake the garden like they did before and not ripen until November? Oh, too late, I see that now. Shit.

Well, what about my paychecks? Are they going to keep coming? From my part-time jobs? From Social Security? My pension? Because how can I live if they don't?

And who is going to deal with stuff that gets left behind when all the Christians are suddenly taken up? Food rotting in the refrigerators, lawns becoming overgrown, their cars sitting in the middle of the road? And who will do their jobs?

Should kids go back to school in September? What about summer vacations? Will there be easier travel? Or will it be worse? Can we just go ahead and max out our credit cards? I mean what's the worst that can happen? Once the Rapture happens, it's for sure the world is going to end, right? No way you're going to be wrong about that part, right? Cause I don't want to be stuck paying off a credit card with 30% interest for the rest of my life.

I know this Harold Camping has been wrong before, but what if he's right this time? He is almost 90, and old people sometimes get things right. You never know.

Let me know if you have more information than I do. You people out in the Midwest seem to be better informed.

Love,
Sandra

Air Pollution

The occasion of the lunar eclipse was
auspicious. My hair was flawless, and
my date was giving me palpitations.

Nothing could go awry.

As we lay in the hammock, gazing at
the sky, I felt more than savvy. At the
moment I intuited the time was right,

I leaned in for a kiss. She offered me
a peppermint.

New Lovers Say Goodbye

See ya later, alligator,
After while, crocodile.

Later, patater.
See ya, wouldn't wanna be ya!

Miss ya, wouldn't wanna
kiss ya!

Ciao, baby . . .
So long, cowpoke.

Y'all come back now, ya hear?
Buh Bye.

Bye bye, baby, goodbye.
Goodbye.

See ya!
Bye now!

Take care.
Catch ya later.

Gotta run.
Okay, bye!

Via con Dios, muchacha.
Adios!

Au 'voir!

Buenas nochas!

Goodnight.
Night night.

Night! I'd better go.
You first.

Non, Merci

I wear my goggles *pour vous* as I ride behind you on your
    bicyclette
pushing my gut into the small of your back.

You in your tuxedo, I in my *robe de soirée baroque, nous
    avons*
so much fun *je vais pisser.* While I am gone you

reveal your purpose to *mes amis:* you planned to propose
    mariage.
J'ai refuser. J'ai dit bonne nuit.

Translated:

No Thanks

I wear my goggles for you as I ride behind you on your
    bicycle
pushing my gut into the small of your back.

You in your tuxedo, I in my baroque evening gown, we
    have
so much fun I had to go pee. While I am gone you

reveal your purpose to my friends: you planned to propose
    marriage.
I refused. I said good night.

HOLIDAYS

Holy Days

My friend John, a holdover from the
union of older men who trained hard to
be curmudgeons, he looks like Santa

and celebrates only Christmas this time of
year. He withholds his Happy New Years
to mean the entire year, not one evening
that can be shrugged off. He casts

aspersions on Saturnalia, Solstice, Kwanza
celebrations as made up reasons to ignore
the true reason for the season.

I may be a bowsprit, poking his well buttressed
defense against what he thinks are pretenders,
but I've waded into his jungle of protestations

to teach him a lesson. Each day I've greeted him
with symbols of Hanukkah, Winter Solstice, Saturnalia,
and today: The Night of the Radishes.

John hollered Uncle a few days ago, but I
won't stop until I tell him
Happy New Year!

'Tis the Season

This is the season for greeting
people with holiday cheer, no
matter how one feels.

Merry Christmas, Happy: Holidays,
Hanukkah, Kwanzaa, New Year,
Solstice.

Shop for wishes, dreams, gifts to
bestow upon clearly disappointed
receivers.

Knit sweaters for family, friends,
pets. Decorate your home with
traditions.

Never mind your aging body filled
with aches, pains, disorientation. It's
the season of joy.

The season of deterioration is year
round. Try to be glad you're alive
to see another December.

Our First Tree

If you will permit me to change one
thing, I believe I can illustrate an
enormous overhaul to the look of this

evergreen. I know you're a minimalist, and
we don't have to have lights, garlands,
tinsel, ornaments, popcorn, cranberries,

or icicles. But putting a simple skirt at the
bottom does not a Christmas tree make.
Can I just, will you let me, may I simply

add a bit of ribbon?

I Wrote to Santa

Today I wrote with an ergonomic
graphite pencil to that pagan god:

Santa. I have no rights here, I'm
way too old to believe in him and

his supernatural ability to deliver the
goods. The very idea is surreal. But,

I'm at my wits' end. How else can I
obtain what I need to jumpstart the

rest of my life? I tried and failed the
Kickstarter program. Begging on the

street is humbling and no one gives
to a fat woman. I figure Santa and I

are about the same size. Maybe he'll
feel empathy and bring me the one

I want. The one I will share my dish
of sherbet with, the one who will

give as much love and support as
I do. The one who is ready to step

into legal same sex marriage with me
and promise till death do us part.

If You Can't Beat 'Em, Join 'Em

Shipping gifts I bought on sale to my
loved ones—scattered across the face of
this planet—is one example of the lengths

I go to in order to avoid feeling isolated.
Others seem to frolic in numerous
parties, events, soirees. Media of every

kind: social, broadcast, artistic, all diverge
from their regular programming to bring
us this seasonal holiday. Well-wishers and

liars alike are shouting greetings to each
and every one of us. If we don't respond in
kind, we're deemed scrooges, grouches,

grinches, or worse. Even the most
depressed among us are urged to cheer
the hell up. Bah humbug? No. Bring it on.

ON A
PERSONAL NOTE

When My Ship Comes In

I will be as patient as my mother was
impatient. My ship will be as laden with goods
as our cupboards at home were bare.

My ship will be as welcoming as my hometown
was intolerant. Its decks as expansive and
clean as the minds of my community were

narrow and dirty. When my ship comes in
it will wait for me to gather my family, my
friends, my community, my frenemies, my
enemies, everyone I've ever met, and

everyone I've never met, and all those who
aren't yet born. We'll jump on that boat
with glee and goodwill. We'll feed the hungry,

tend the sick, honor the aged, rock
the babies, slake all our thirst and sing praise
to the universe of which we are all one.

We will set sail to see the world by day
and by star-filled night, blessing the fishes
and animals of the sea, kissing

the denizens of the air with our lips
and our eyes, until the end of time.

The Royal We

We must have been afraid to know
the truth, because we waited until
we were home from the doctor to
check our left breast.

Our doctor doesn't like to touch people.
Eleven years without a breast exam. Eleven
years without a skin check for cancer. She's
a wizard at staying abreast on medicine, but
she never touches if she can help it.

Yesterday we went in because we've
been sweating like a stevedore wearing
fur in the summer in Arizona. Doctor
ordered five million blood tests, listened
to our heart through our shirt, and
gave reassurances.

Then before we went to bed, we found
the lump. When we called for another
appointment, we asked for someone
willing to place hands on.

The Really Big Show

In a show of faith in myself, I purchased
pink cowboy boots to wear to Austin. My
director chose red. We were going to
Texas to kick ass with my script.

We made the short list, but didn't
win.

The boots were made of Italian leather,
comfortable on my feet, easy on my eyes.
But something was off.

Those pink boots seemed to say
"short list" "short list" with every
step I took.

Short list still means no. I gave
the damned boots away. They were
kicking my ass.

Watch the Birdie

She was invited to play a gigantic game of badminton
but didn't take it literally. She thought they meant

the game would run long. She had a venti latte, wore her
strappiest sandals and cutest sporty outfit and

hopped the train for Cornwall. She arrived in time for
elevenses, headed to the strand with her picnic basket

and fainted dead away when she caught sight of the
leviathan in whites swatting an enormous birdie over

a net the entire length of the county. When she came
to, she realized the birdie was merely a statue

And, she needed to eat.

Lost

Sometimes things in my house   go missing
They are not lost   or mislaid

In my house   there are no   little people
no goblins that'll get you   iff'n you   don't watch out

Items   slip   into   another
                                dimension.

Somehow   there is a   shift.
Maybe it is the wind.   Or maybe something more
            subtle.

A tone.   Radiation levels.   A rise in
barometric pressure.

An object will   suddenly   shift into
the fourth dimension.

I search for it. Sometimes for minutes, sometimes for
days. In the same places, over and over. Where it was,
where it is supposed to be. And then, it
                reappears.   Bam.

Back again.

As if it had been lost   or even abducted,   or possibly
                liberated.

Wrapping to Go

Wear this, it's cold out. I don't want
you to catch your death.

Take these leftovers home with you, use
the plastic.

Mom, do you have anything? Maddy has a
party to go to, and I'm all out.

Keep your baking dishes clean. Use the
aluminum, or baker's paper.

My house is full: sweaters, shawls, jackets, scarves.
Christmas, birthday, congratulations, all-occasion.

Cling, waxed, shiny on one side, cellophane, cupcake
    liners,
or parchment. I can wrap anything and take it to go.

Bandana Blouse

Simple to make, Mom said.
Take two bandanas, sew them
up the sides, leave holes

for your arms, sew across
the top, leave a hole big enough
for your head. What could be

easier? Really, for once my
Mom was right. Now that I
was twelve, I found Mom

was wrong most of the time,
but this sounded like a piece
of cake. I found two red

bandanas, and went to the
basement, opened the garage
door to the outside, in order

to keep an eye on my
little sister, dragged the
treadle machine across

the floor and got situated. Wait.
For some reason, machine
wants to sew only one stitch

at a time. I fiddle, and look,
turn buttons and growl, all
for nothing. Determined and patient.

I sew my new blouse stitch by
single stitch. All afternoon.

Finally, I'm ready just minutes
before Mom comes home.
I'm proud of my accomplishment.

Mom says, all you had to do
was tighten up the screw
after you filled the bobbin.

I could tell she liked my
new blouse.

The Cost of Living

It's no exaggeration to say I prefer
no sudden noises, no changes to my agenda,
no stabbing pains, nothing to rock my boat,

nothing to strip away my façade of calm.
I prefer rules I can mold to suit my life,
in fact, I'd like to carry them in plaster

to the foundry, have them cast in bronze,
hang them on the wall for all to follow.

But, as it happens, I'm living in the
current world. Maybe even the real
one. Change is the only constant.

Rules are fluid. Noise is the music of life.
Pain is a reminder of existence. Reality
inserts itself at every opportunity.

My agenda is the apple pie, and reality
is the topping, where nothing is
à la mode.

Not Fitting In

Where all the ceilings are extremely
low, almost every person in my
family feels entirely fine. Mom said
I was a throwback, some ancestor or
other must have been tall.

In the real world, I'm a little above
average, but I didn't start out this
way. I was the shortest girl in every
class until my sophomore year. Encouraged
by the growth spurt, I went on to grow
two more inches. I no longer fit in my
family home.

The sink was so low, I got a backache
from doing dishes. Beds were close to
the floor and I could barely get out of
them, let alone bend to make them.

Chairs, tables, everything was short. A
ladder was required by everyone but
me to reach the cupboards, the books
on the shelves. Even the ladder was
short.

Mom stored items of all stripes and
sizes on the floor. I would walk around
searching for a magazine, the newspaper,
her glasses, and all the time they were
in a stack on the floor.

It was painful to me to visit, so I
never stayed long. And as I left
I bumped my head on the door.

Mirror, Mirror

You capture every spark of
light in the room and send it

to another corner. You show
me what I might look like in

a reverse universe, keeping my
actual likeness to yourself. You

shine, even in the night, reminding
me of your everlasting presence.

Without saying a word, you
light up the dark.

Grandma Tells Me How to Find Salvation

God's in the details, Sis, that's
all I know. So if you're looking for

salvation I suggest you stop gazing out
the window and get down on your

hands and knees with that rag and
scrub the floors until them details

are visible. When I and your old
grandpa could join you for some

supper on that floor with nary a
one of us getting sick from it

why God would bless us
everyone.

And ain't that enough
salvation for ye?

Golden Gate

I pity every person who has never visited the City
by the Bay, who never had a chance to leave her
heart or a piece of it in San Francisco.

I pity those who've never seen the corner of Haight
and Ashbury, worn flowers in her hair, dined in
　　Chinatown,

driven down or hiked up the curviest street in the world.
Who wouldn't want to see the murals of Coit Tower,

or stand in the aisle of the church where Marilyn wed Joe?
Even if your heart ached knowing the pain she suffered

at his hands, and the heartache he felt after she was
gone. I've never lived on Valencia Street, but I've

performed there. I've slept in beds all over the
city. Oakland too. Travelled on BART, rode past

my stop on a holiday. Missed breakfast due to
daydreaming until I was under the bay. San Francisco

is a magical city with mild winters and cold foggy
summers, diverse neighborhoods, block parties,

farmer's markets that sell bonsai plants, and some
of my best friends.

But you know that world famous Golden Gate?
It's orange.

Why I Should Never Shop at Saks

A brief encounter with a pair of gloves
shouldn't leave me feeling shaken, but it has.

No one has the right to own something
like this. Do they?

What are they made of? They feel like
baby's skin, like an infant's underarm,

where the softest part of the body
has never seen the light, or felt

the rigors of weather. Inside and out,
the leather is better than my own skin.

These gloves make me want to rob a bank,
or kill my rich uncle so I can purchase them.

I don't have a rich uncle and I don't
own a gun, so everyone can stand down.

But I have to have those gloves.
I wonder. Can I get them in gray?

Elevators in Dreams

What was Mr. Otis thinking when he created
elevators for dreams? They never work right.

They go sideways for miles at a time, flying up
and over trains or wet fields. They stop between

floors, miss floors altogether, fly up
and down at speeds not allowed even

on the autobahn. Worse yet I get in
one elevator and end up in another

in a mall across the highway on a floor
that won't allow me to get to my

baby stranded at the stroller park or
my dying grandmother I left outside

the emergency room while I parked
my car. When I try to get back in

the buttons don't work, the elevator
is filled with people in a hurry to get

somewhere else entirely. Stairs would
be better if I could find them. Phones

don't work, I can't wake up, and all
I can do is try another elevator.

Learning Italian

Tonight when I go to a place down the street,
I'm going to order off the menu. Act as if

I know the chef, or perhaps am one myself. I'll have
Erbazzone con scarola to start, *Garganelli fatto a mano*

witha San Marzano tomato cream
sauce, *Insalata di asparagi bianchik.*

I'll skip the main course tonight,
and for dessert, bring me *Formaggi, due o tre.*

I hope the pizzeria doesn't
throw me out.

That's Hot

When I came out as a lesbian, a friend recommended
a women's festival in the Ozarks.

There, not everyone was nude, because any amount
of clothing was optional. I wore no top.

One young woman walked around in a dress with buttons
down the front—but only the top two were done up.

Some women wore nothing at all for the entire seven days.
Others were covered, wearing even socks and shoes.

I found the experience delicious—like sipping chocolate.
Never gulping, ever mindful of not burning my tongue.

Sense of Smell

We McCorkle sisters were born with an acute sense of
    smell.
We might have been dogs in a prior life. No one had to tell
    us

to follow our nose. It was a curse I thought everyone was
    born with,
until sometime in my grown life I realized it was only my
    sister and me.

She walked into my house one time and sniffed out a
    marijuana roach
I didn't know was there. But either one of us could find a
    restroom

from half a mile away, tell when our friends were on their
    periods,
know when the cake was ready to come out of the oven
    without looking,

and were both intolerant of body odor and bad breath.
    Kissing was always
problematic for me. I wanted to kiss, but oh, the lingering
    smells of garlic,

onions, even things like Juicy Fruit gum. Mint was an
    assault that
drove sharp spikes up through my nasal passages to my
    tear ducts.

How did others not cry over breath fresheners? Peri-
    menopause
brought a blessing disguised as a hallucination: I thought
    the house was on fire.

Or the car. Or maybe the office. I could smell burning
    dust. Everywhere.
Several days and nights each month. Sometimes it woke
    me from a sound

sleep and I leaped from my bed, turned on the lights and
    scrambled around
the house checking for smoke. No smoke, no fire.

Eventually, it burned itself out. And left me with a much
    diminished sense of smell.
I imagine myself to be normal now.

True Story

When I was a kid I read everything, including the
    magazines
True Confessions, *True Romance*, and my favorite: *True
    Story*.

I would read them and think, I could write this shit. Later
    I learned
all those true stories were made up. True story.

The story of my life in *True Story* story titles: I Was
    Pregnant
and Married at Fifteen! My Husband Beats Me, and I Stay!

I Cheated on My Air Force Husband! My Married Lover's
    Wife Turned Me
Into a Lesbian! I Married a Monster—He Raped
    Everybody! True story.

After that I couldn't look at another magazine. Couldn't
    face another fake
true story. I finished college, came out, took up theater,
    started writing for real,

telling stories with truth. No shit.

Do Jump! Theatre

The daring woman on her trapeze is
standing, flying, hanging by her feet.

She flips up and over, around. She climbs

the silks to the very ceiling, opens a trap
door and disappears inside it. We in the audience

are enraptured. More women appear. More trapezes
appear. Women are zipping, diving, swinging everywhere.

I think I might expire.

The lights dim. The first woman returns. With another
    woman,
they soar together. Projections and music set the scene

for romance. I am entranced. I may run away and
join the circus.

About the Poet

Sandra de Helen published her first poem at the age of fourteen. Her English teacher, Janice Wallace, submitted the poem to a teacher's magazine and surprised Sandra with a copy in print. The poem was about abortion, which was illegal at the time.

In her twenties, Sandra published a few poems in newspapers, which spurred her to take a Creative Writing Class at the local community college. The [male] professor professed she would never make a good poet because she didn't "write like a man." The next year she joined the women's movement and turned to writing plays.

Forty years later, she picked up Sage Cohen's book, *Writing the Life Poetic: An Invitation to Read and Write Poetry*, and resumed writing poems like a woman.

A long-time resident of Portland, Oregon, Sandra recently relocated to sunny California where she lives with her daughter and a very special cat.

Praise for Other Works by Sandra de Helen

Poetry

"[The poems in *All This Remains to be Discovered*] are a vulnerable, raw look at one's life with an undertone of tenderness and adult compassion and forgiveness. A very moving and worthwhile read."
~BuzzOregon

"I loved how honest and plain all the tales were [in *All This Remains to be Discovered*]. After reading this short book, I felt like I knew, intimately, every important person in the poet's life."
~Amazon.com

Plays

"[The stageplay] *The Clue in the Old Birdbath* is proving to be catnip for the robust, unadorned, unescorted females in attendance. Unfolding is a musical demolition by Sandra de Helen and Kate Kasten of Carolyn Keene's nubile teen detective Nancy Drew, here renamed Tansy True. Here, adolescent literature's beacon of girlish pluck and ingenuity is rendered into a salty, torpedo-breasted assassin of male domination."
~Keith A. Joseph, Cleveland Scene

Novels

"I wish I had half the plotting talent that Sandra de Helen has. [*Till Darkness Comes*] is such a terrific and totally satisfying book."
~Chelsea Cain, Thriller Writer, Humorist, and News Columnist

"[*The Hounding* is a] confident, meticulously detailed mystery that would have made Shirley [Comb's] pipe-smoking idol proud."
~Kirkus Reviews

"*The Hounding* is . . . an interesting and well-developed mystery. I recommend it for any Holmes/Watson obsessives."
~Megan Casey, Lesbrary.com

"If you are a lover of Sherlock Holmes, [*The Illustrious Client*] is a fun look at what might happen had the characters been women and in the present day. The books' titles are taken from Sherlock Holmes' own stories and this book is loosely based on the one of the same title. However, this is not just a retelling of the Holmes stories. Ms. de Helen definitely makes it her own. The clues and red herrings as the pair solve the mystery are well placed. The plot was strong and interesting, and like a really good mystery, I couldn't figure out 'whodunnit' and was surprised by the reveal at the end."
~Long and Short Reviews.com

"[*The Illustrious Client*] is certainly worth a read. With the author continuing to hone her talents, I am looking forward to the next one."
~Megan Casey, Lesbrary.com

www.ingramcontent.com/pod-product-compliance
Lightning Source LLC
Chambersburg PA
CBHW030214130726
47898CB00012B/1022